Havok and Wolverine: Meltdown. Originally published as Havok & Wolverine:
Meltdown #1-4. Published by Epic Comics, 387 Park Avenue South, New
York, NY 10016. Copyright © 1989, 1990 Marvel Entertainment Group,
Inc. All rights reserved. Havok and Wolverine and all prominent characters
appearing herein and the distinctive likenesses thereof are trademarks of
Epic Comics. No part of this book may be printed or reproduced in any
manner without the written permission of the publisher. Printed in the
U.S.A. First Printing: 1990. ISBN# 0-87135-700-3

10 9 8 7 6 5 4 3 2 1

" THE **ATOM**, GENERAL MELTDOWN, IS THE HEART OF THE MATTER.

" ONCE, IT WAS THOUGHT TO BE INDESTRUCTABLE, IMMUTABLE, ETERNAL.

" WE KNOW BETTER NOW.

" OR WORSE, DEPENDING ON YOUR POINT OF VIEW.

" WE KNOW NOW THAT ATOMS CAN BE BROKEN.

" INTO FRAGMENTS
AND ENERGY. "

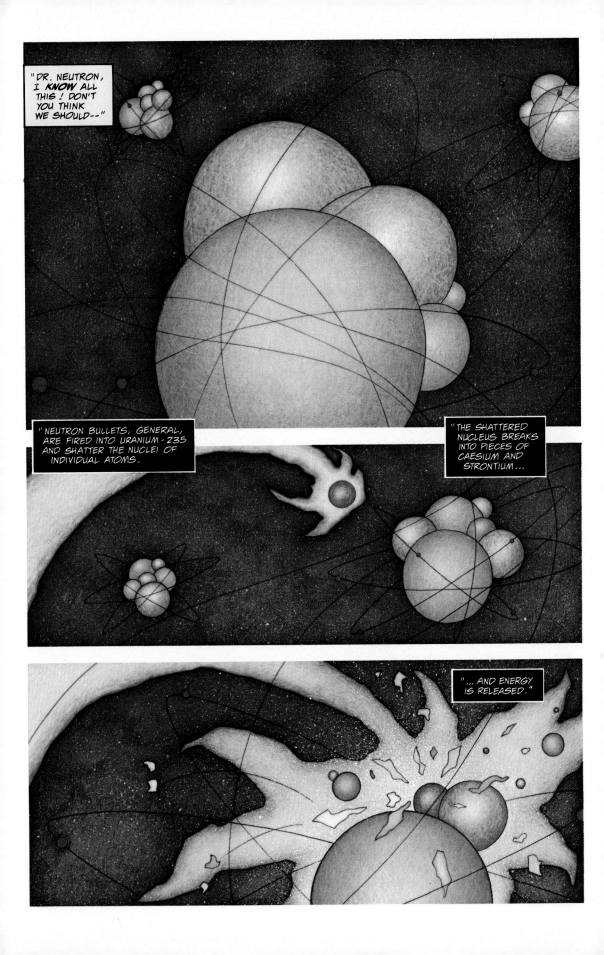

"A GREAT DEAL OF ENERGY.

"SO A MODERATOR, IN THIS CASE A GRAPHITE DRUM, IS USED TO SLOW THE NEUTRONS DOWN.

"BORON STEEL CONTROL RODS ABSORB SOME OF THE NEUTRONS TO REGULATE THE SPEED OF THE REACTION.

"NUCLEAR FISSION PRODUCES ENOUGH ENERGY TO POWER A SUBMARINE...

"...TO LIGHT A CITY... OR DESTROY A WORLD.

"THE ANNUAL MAINTENANCE SHUTDOWN OF THE RBMK-1000·REACTOR NO. 4 AT THE CHERNOBYL POWER STATION WAS **TO** BE THE **PERFECT** OPPORTUNITY."

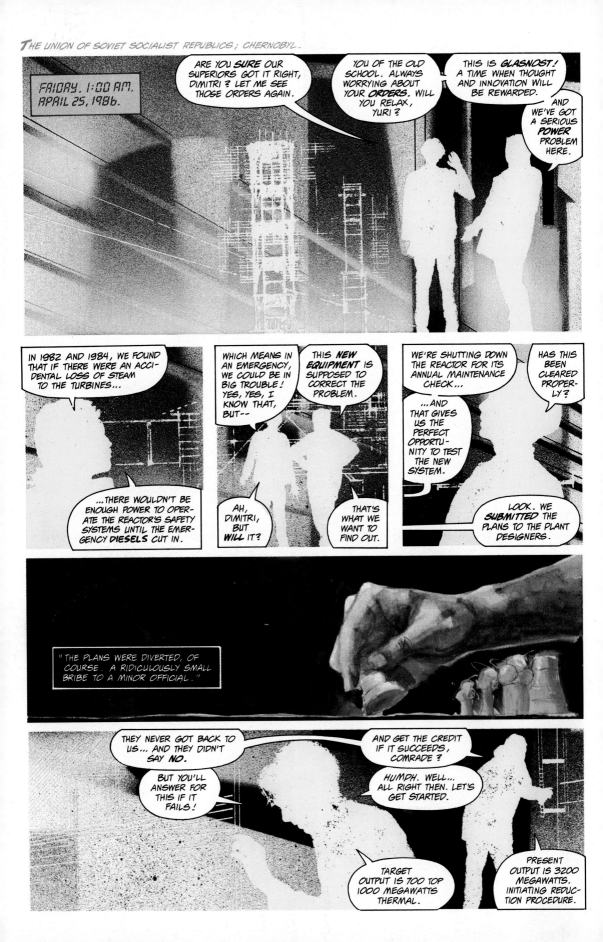

FRIDAY. 1:00 AM.
APRIL 25, 1986.

ARE YOU **SURE** OUR SUPERIORS GOT IT RIGHT, DIMITRI? LET ME SEE THOSE ORDERS AGAIN.

YOU OF THE OLD SCHOOL. ALWAYS WORRYING ABOUT YOUR **ORDERS**. WILL YOU RELAX, YURI?

THIS IS **GLASNOST!** A TIME WHEN THOUGHT AND INNOVATION WILL BE REWARDED.

AND WE'VE GOT A SERIOUS **POWER** PROBLEM HERE.

IN 1982 AND 1984, WE FOUND THAT IF THERE WERE AN ACCIDENTAL LOSS OF STEAM TO THE TURBINES...

...THERE WOULDN'T BE ENOUGH POWER TO OPERATE THE REACTOR'S SAFETY SYSTEMS UNTIL THE EMERGENCY **DIESELS** CUT IN.

WHICH MEANS IN AN EMERGENCY, WE COULD BE IN BIG TROUBLE! YES, YES, I KNOW THAT, BUT--

THIS **NEW EQUIPMENT** IS SUPPOSED TO CORRECT THE PROBLEM.

AH, DIMITRI, BUT **WILL** IT?

THAT'S WHAT WE WANT TO FIND OUT.

WE'RE SHUTTING DOWN THE REACTOR FOR ITS ANNUAL MAINTENANCE CHECK...

...AND THAT GIVES US THE PERFECT OPPORTUNITY TO TEST THE NEW SYSTEM.

HAS THIS BEEN CLEARED PROPERLY?

LOOK. WE **SUBMITTED** THE PLANS TO THE PLANT DESIGNERS.

"THE PLANS WERE DIVERTED, OF COURSE. A RIDICULOUSLY SMALL BRIBE TO A MINOR OFFICIAL."

THEY NEVER GOT BACK TO US... AND THEY DIDN'T **SAY NO**.

BUT YOU'LL ANSWER FOR THIS IF IT FAILS!

AND GET THE CREDIT IF IT SUCCEEDS, COMRADE?

HUMPH. WELL... ALL RIGHT THEN. LET'S GET STARTED.

TARGET OUTPUT IS 700 TOP 1000 MEGAWATTS THERMAL.

PRESENT OUTPUT IS 3200 MEGAWATTS. INITIATING REDUCTION PROCEDURE.

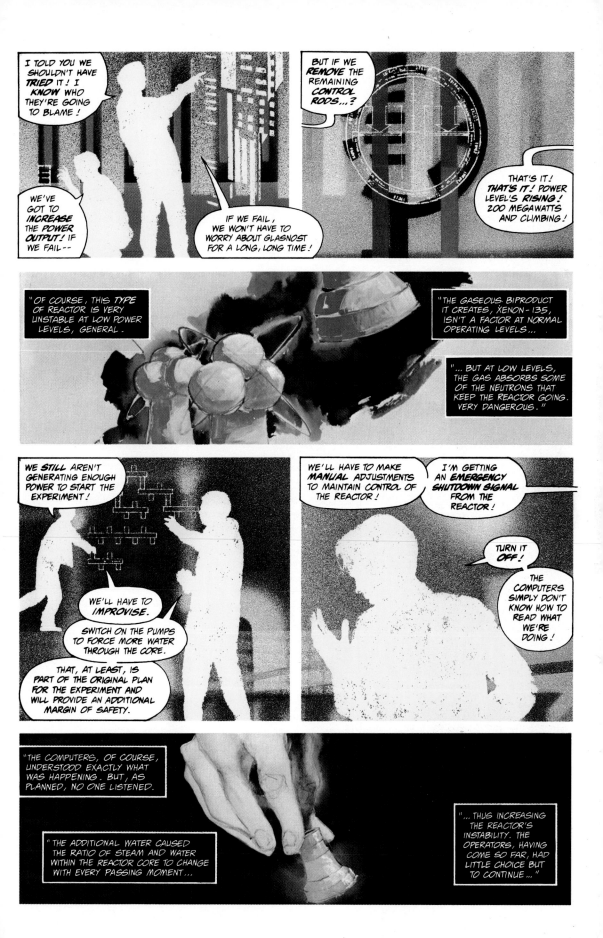

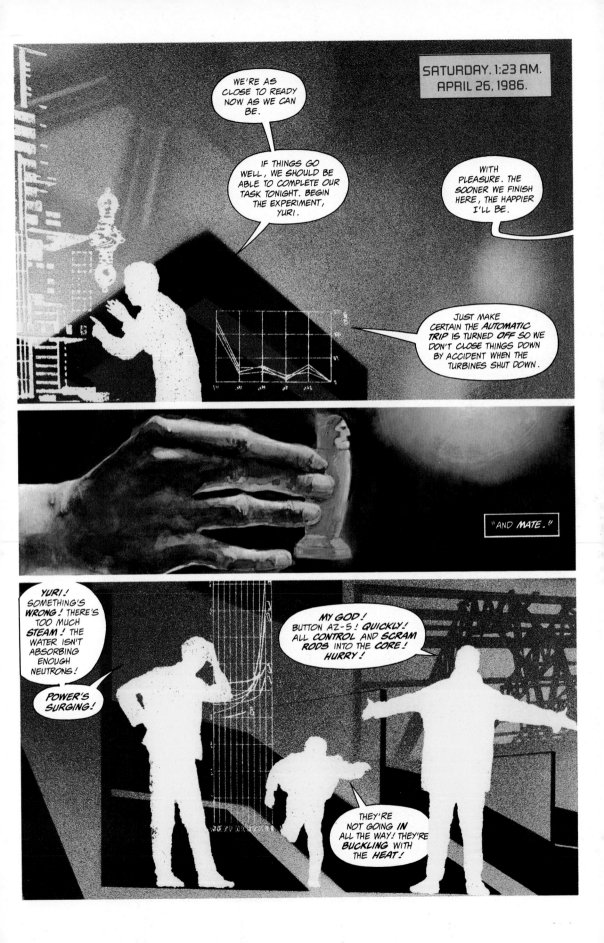

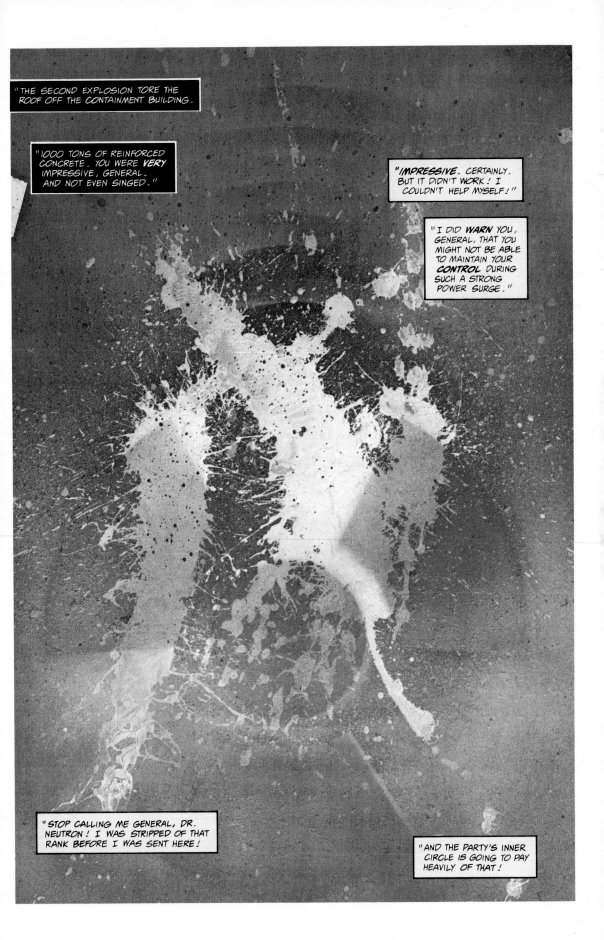

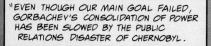

"EVEN THOUGH OUR MAIN GOAL FAILED, GORBACHEV'S CONSOLIDATION OF POWER HAS BEEN SLOWED BY THE PUBLIC RELATIONS DISASTER OF CHERNOBYL.

"IT IS A START!

"AND THE NEXT TIME, WE WILL STRIKE HARD ENOUGH TO BRING DOWN THIS MAN AND HIS CRIPPLING POLICIES...

"...THAT THREATEN TO REDUCE OUR NATION TO A PEACELOVING, SECOND-RATE POWER!"

"NO DOUBT, GENERAL, WHEN YOU ARE IN CHARGE, THINGS WILL BE *DIFFERENT*.

"AT LEAST WE KNOW NOW THAT THIS APPROACH *DISPERSES* THE RADIATION TOO WIDELY FOR DIRECT ABSORPTION.

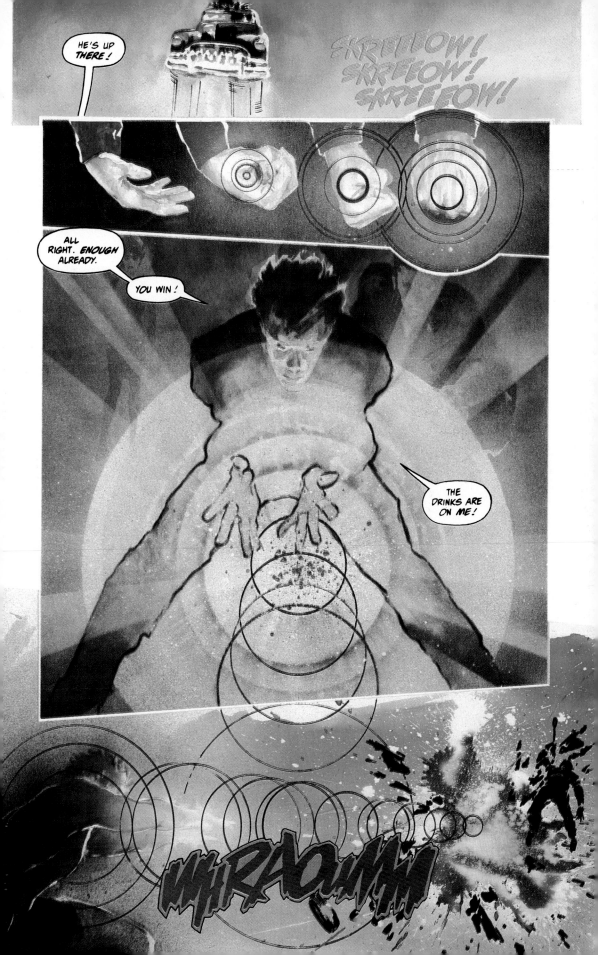

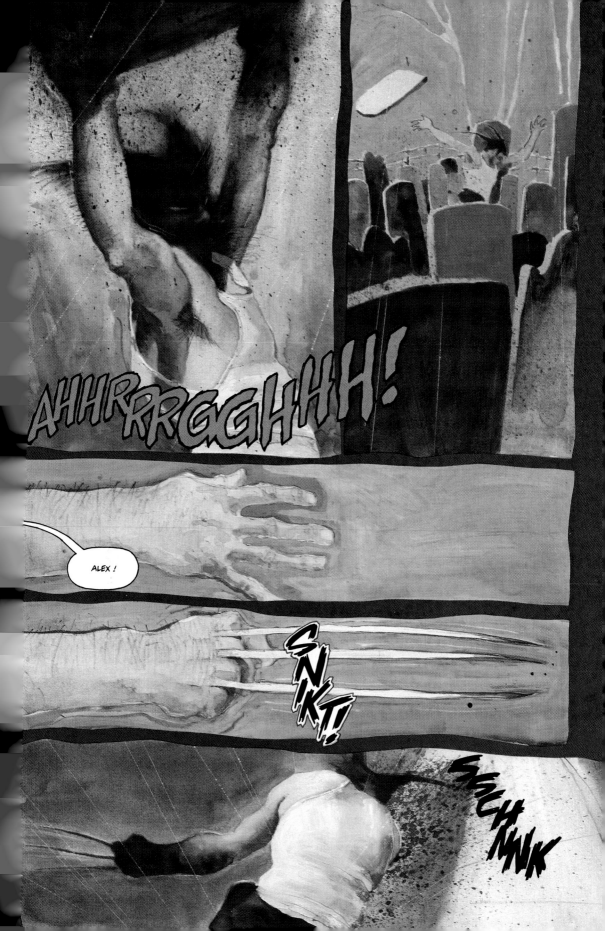

TENDER LOVING
A CÃNTINA ON THE EASTERN COAST OF MEXICO. LESS THAN A WEEK AGO, IT WAS THE SCENE OF A BRAWL TO END ALL BRAWLS.
NOW WOLVERINE IS BACK, AND HE WANTS JUST ONE THING... INFORMATION.
THE MEN MY FRIEND AND I FOUGHT FOLLOWED US BACK TO OUR HOTEL ROOM AND ATTACKED US THERE.
WHERE CAN I FIND THESE MEN?

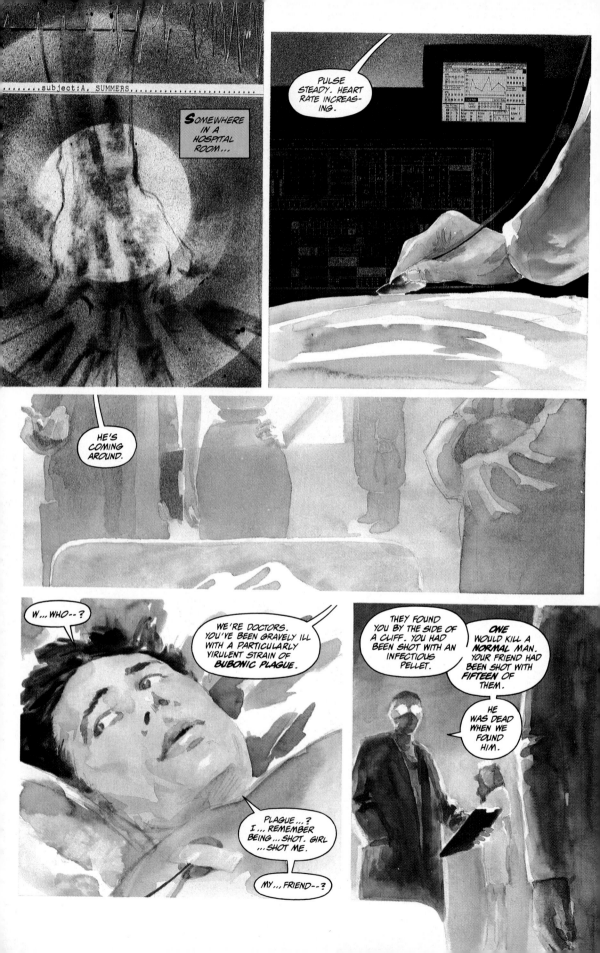

"YES. WE MUST MONITOR *BOTH* OF THEM ... MOST *CAREFULLY*-"

THOUSANDS MARCHED IN PROTEST OF THE OPENING OF THE NUCLEAR REACTOR IN ISRAEL ...

...TOO SIMILAR IN DESIGN, MANY CITIZENS FEEL, TO THE RUSSIAN CHERNOBYL FACILITY.

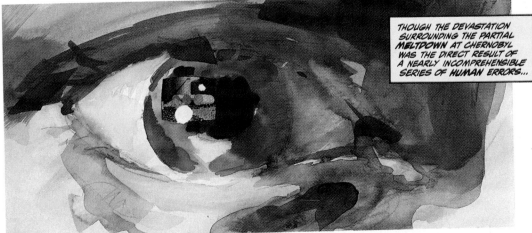

THOUGH THE DEVASTATION SURROUNDING THE PARTIAL MELTDOWN AT CHERNOBYL WAS THE DIRECT RESULT OF A NEARLY INCOMPREHENSIBLE SERIES OF HUMAN ERRORS...

rrmmmm

THE HOTEL MARIMBA ON THE OUTSKIRTS OF TOWN. IT IS NO LONGER THE SEASON FOR TOURISTS AND ITS SINGLE GRINGO GUEST, **LOGAN** ON THE REGISTER, HAS TURNED IN FOR THE NIGHT...

WOLVERINE HASN'T BEEN TOO CAREFUL DURING HIS STAY IN MEXICO.

:snap:

HE HAS MADE ENEMIES.

KA-CHUNK!

THUMP THUD THUMP THUD THUMP THUD THUMP THUD THUMP THUD

SLAMM

IT'S ONE OF THE THINGS HE DOES BEST.

...COULD SNEAK HIM IN HERE. IT **WORKED**, ALEX. WE ACTUALLY **TRICKED** HIM. HE'S HERE!

SLAM

I DON'T HAVE MUCH TIME, SUMMERS, SO WE'LL MAKE THIS SHORT AND SWEET.

I'M LOOKING FOR A MAN NAMED **LOGAN**. WHAT DO YOU KNOW ABOUT HIM?

THE DOCTORS TOLD ME THAT LOGAN WAS **DEAD**.

WE'VE CHECKED. HIS DEATH WAS FAKED.

NORMALLY, I'D ENJOY DANCING WITH YOU ABOUT THIS, BUT THIS IS A MATTER OF **NATIONAL SECURITY**.

YOU ... YOU *HIT* HIM. HE'S OUT *COLD*.

YEAH ... WELL ... WHERE I COME FROM, WE LEARNED *SELF DEFENSE* ALONGSIDE READIN', WRITIN' AND 'RITHMATIC.

YOU'RE *SHAKING*. AND YOUR LIP'S *BLEEDING*.

IT'S *NOTHING*. IT'S JUST THAT I'M NOT *USED*--

IT'LL *STOP*.

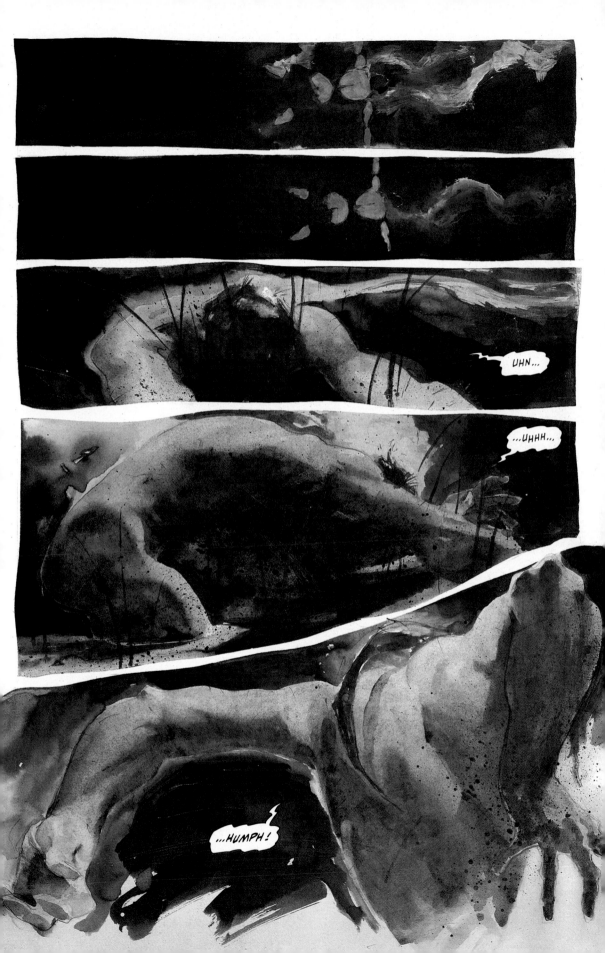

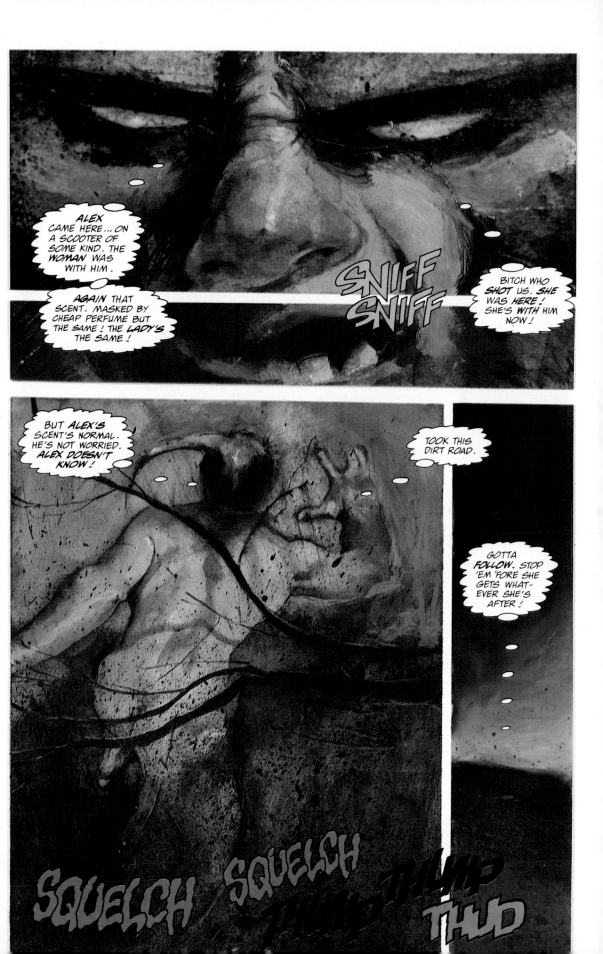

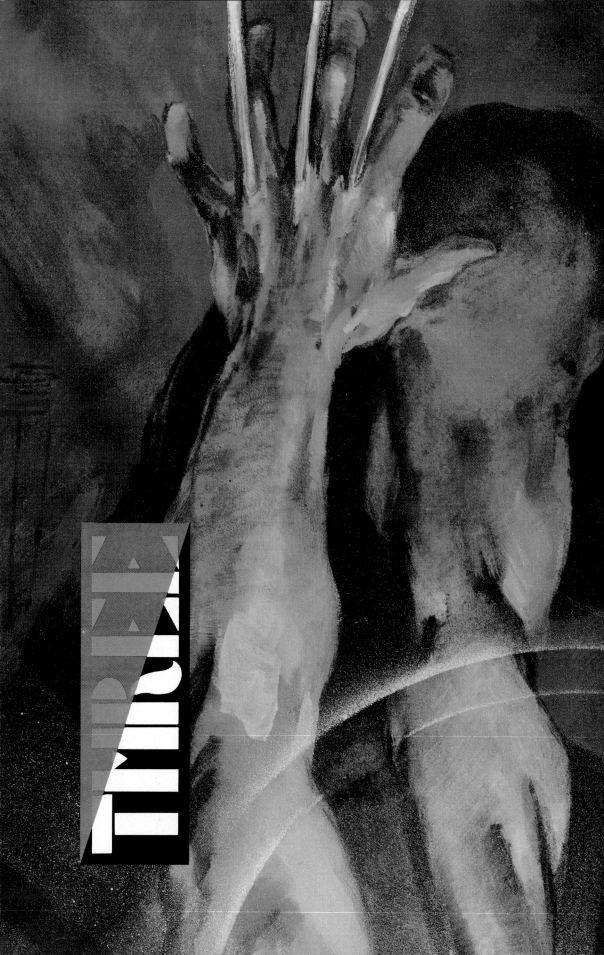

THREE

duel

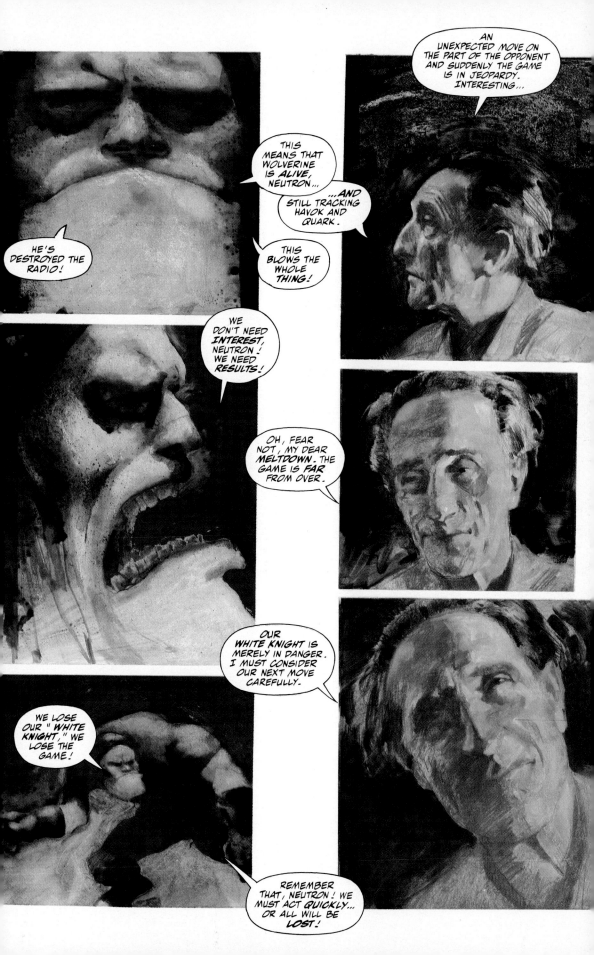

EVERY SECOND COUNTS NOW.
IT'S A CINCH WHOEVER'S GOT ALEX IS GONNA GET HIM OUT OF HERE AS FAST AS POSSIBLE!
WHUPWHUPWH
AN' I'LL BET MY LAST BEER THAT LITTLE BIMBETTE IS LEADIN' HIM BY THE NOSE!
WELL, DON'T START COUNTIN' ANY CHICKENS, LADY.
ALEX MAY BE TOO YOUNG TA KNOW ANY BETTER, BUT OL' LOGAN'S BEEN AROUND THE TRACK MORE THAN ONCE.
WHUP WHUP WHUP WHUP WHUP WHUP WHUP

SIBERIA. THE GULAG. BENEATH THE INSANE ASYLUM THAT IS MELTDOWN'S SECRET HEAD-QUARTERS, THE ELEVATOR SHAFT PLUNGES TEN THOUSAND FEET THROUGH SOLID ROCK.

THERE, DOWN A STEEL-WALLED HALLWAY, SURROUNDED BY A SERIES OF RADIATION PROOF SHIELDS, IS MELTDOWN'S LEAD-LINED *WORKOUT ROOM* ... THE ONE PLACE IN ALL THE WORLD WHERE HE CAN PUT RESTRAINT ASIDE AND SIMPLY BE ... HIMSELF.

THAT A CAPITALIST *PIGMY* SHOULD *LEARN* OF OUR PLAN IS INEX-CUSABLE.

THAT HE DARES DEFY TH MIGHT OF MOTHER RUSS AND *LIVE* IS *UNFORGIV-ABLE!*

THAT HE DARES *THREATEN* US IS *UNEN-DURABLE!*

ding

WHAT'S *GOOD* ABOUT IT? RAISE THE *RADIATION COLUMN!*

MERIDA IS NOT THE MOST MODERN OF AIRPORTS, BUT THEN, HAVOK HASN'T BEEN FLYING THE MOST MODERN OF AIRPLANES...

WHAT'S GOING ON? THERE'S NOBODY AROUND.

SIESTA TIME.

SOUNDS GREAT, DOESN'T IT? WE COULD BOTH USE THE REST.

YEAH. YOU BEEN REAL SICK AN' FOUGHT THAT SPY AN' FLEW THAT PLANE ALL NIGHT LONG THROUGH A STORM AN'...

LISTEN, ALEX. I GOTTA GO... YOU KNOW ... FRESHEN UP?

YOU MEAN GIRLS STILL REALLY POWDER THEIR NOSES?

WHY DON'T YOU STRETCH OUT ON THE BENCH, SMARTY, AN' TRY AN' GET SOME REST...?

GOOD IDEA!

YES, I UNDERSTAND. THE JET WILL ARRIVE WITHIN A MATTER OF MINUTES.

SPARE ME YOUR CONCERN, COMRADE NEUTRON. I WILL NOT FAIL YOU.

MY QUARRY IS WELL IN HAND.

YOU SEE, ALEX TRUSTS ME. HE DOESN'T SUSPECT THAT HE IS THE ONE WHO HAS, IN EFFECT, BEEN KIDNAPPED!

I'VE PLAYED MY PART... MUCH TOO WELL... FOR THAT.

BUT AS A GESTURE OF GOOD FAITH, NEUTRON, LET ME SUGGEST A WAY IN WHICH WOLVERINE CAN BE PUT TO GOOD USE.

IT BEGINS WITH THE DRESS, WHICH I AM NOW WEARING, AND WHICH I WILL LEAVE BEHIND IN THE LADIES ROOM.

IT SHALL BE THE BAIT THAT WILL ENSNARE OUR RELENTLESS PURSUER...

WAKE UP, SLEEPYHEAD. I GOT GREAT NEWS.

MY FRIEND CHARLIE LEFT A MESSAGE. SAID HE'D BE MORE THAN WILLING TO TAKE US WHEREVER WE WANNA GO...

...LONG AS WE PAY FOR THE PRIVILEGE. ONLY THING IS... WE CAN'T ASK TOO MANY QUESTIONS, O.K.?

HEY, THAT'S GREAT! ALMOST... TOO GREAT. SCARLETT ...THE FIRST GUY...

JOE.

...LOANS YOU HIS PLANE. THE OTHER GUY AGREES TO FLY US TO POLAND.

WHY WOULD YOUR... FRIENDS GO TO ALL THAT TROUBLE?

I WAS... AFRAID YOU'D ASK ME THAT.

ALEX, I'M GONNA TELL YOU THE TRUTH, ONLY YOU GOTTA PROMISE ME YOU WON'T BE MAD, OKAY?

A LONG TIME AGO... JOE... IT'S HIS BI-PLANE... JOE AN' ME, WE WERE... REAL CLOSE.

AN' THEN... THE WAY HE STARTED THROWIN' MONEY AROUND AN' ALL... I THOUGHT, WELL... HE WAS MAYBE RUNNIN' DRUGS.

HE SAID HE WASN'T, BUT I THOUGHT REALLY HE WAS.

SO, I... I STOPPED SEEIN' HIM, BUT... WELL, WHEN YOU WERE IN SUCH BAD TROUBLE, I HADDA DO SOMETHING, DIDN'T I?

I DIDN'T TELL YOU BEFORE. I WAS KINDA ASHAMED... AN' I WAS REAL WORRIED...

I THOUGHT MAYBE IF YOU... KNEW HOW I GOT THE PLANE, YOU MIGHT NOT WANNA USE IT.

BUT CHARLIE... HE'S DIFFERENT. IT'S NOTHING PERSONAL WITH CHARLIE.

ALL HE WANTS IS THE MONEY...!

" IN THE MEANTIME, THANKS TO WOLVERINE, WE SHALL BE ABLE TO LEARN A GREAT DEAL MORE ABOUT THE EFFECTS OF PHOTONIC QUANTUM BRAINWIPING.

"HAVOK'S ENERGY SENSITIVITY UNFORTUNATELY MADE HIM A POOR SUBJECT, BUT WOLVERINE'S REMARKABLE RESILIENCY MAKES HIM AN *EXCELLENT* CHOICE FOR A FULL POWERED EXPERIMENT...

"...THEREBY PROVIDING US WITH A GREAT DEAL OF DATA WE MIGHT NEVER OBTAIN FROM AN ORDINARY HUMAN.

"IN THE END, OF COURSE, WHATEVER DAMAGE HE MAY SUSTAIN WILL BE OF LITTLE CONSEQUENCE SINCE HE IS ALREADY AS GOOD AS DEAD.

"NOTIFY DUBINSKY. THEY ARE TO ADJUST THE HELMET TO RADIATE A TOTAL BRAINWIPE, LEAVING ONLY THE INSTRUCTIONS WE REQUIRE."

IN THE SHADOWS OF THE CARPATHIA MOUNTAINS...

ENDGAME

SOMEONE WHO WANTED HIM TO GET TO ME!

BUT I GOT TO HIM INSTEAD!

HE WAS MY FRIEND... AND I KILLED HIM!

WHY? I KEEP ASKING MYSELF WHY... AND IT DOESN'T MAKE ANY SENSE!

WHO WOULD WANT ME DEAD... AND AT HIS HANDS?

COMPLETE WITH POWER OUTPUT TABLES, THERMONUCLEAR REAC-TION CHARTS, STUFF ABOUT PLANT SECURITY...

NOTATIONS SUGGEST THAT IT'S DUE TO BE SHUT DOWN FOR ANNUAL MAINTEN-ANCE IN A FEW DAYS...

...WHICH MEANS IT WILL BE OPERATING WITH A SKELETON CREW...

...AND A REDUCED LEVEL OF SECURITY.

THIS MIGHT EXPLAIN WHY SOMEBODY WANTS ME OUT OF THE WAY.

WHATEVER SKULLDUGGERY IS BEING PLANNED AT THE PLANT...

...MY MUTANT ABILITY TO ABSORB ENERGY COULD STOP IT.

MAYBE THEY WANTED ME OUT OF THE WAY PERMANENTLY!

BUT THEY WANTED IT TO LOOK LIKE AN ACCIDENT.

NO EMBARASSING QUESTIONS OR OFFICIAL INVEST-IGATIONS.

SO THAT'S WHY THEY SHOT YOU WITH THAT PLAGUE VIRUS...

....AND WHEN THAT DIDN'T WORK...

INDIA, THE DISTRICT OF MAHARASHTRA, NOT FAR FROM THE TARAPUR NUCLEAR REACTOR...

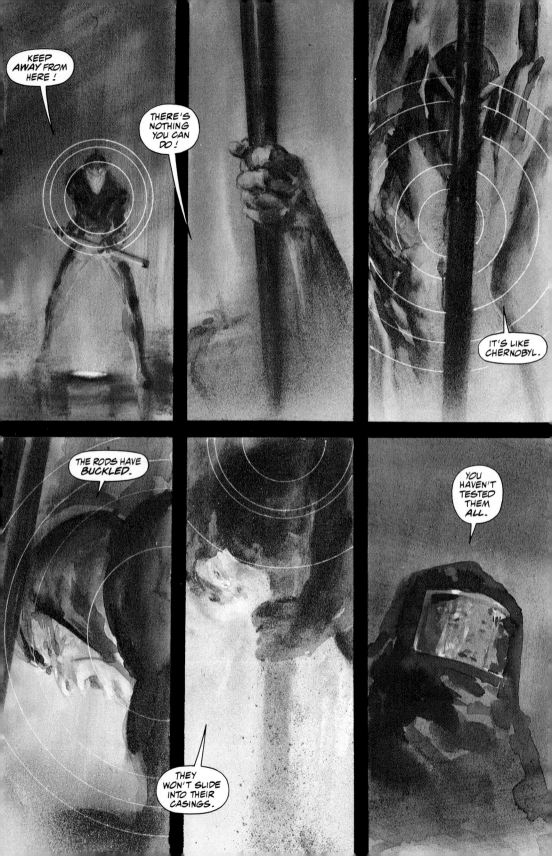

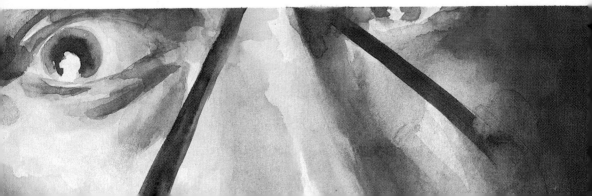

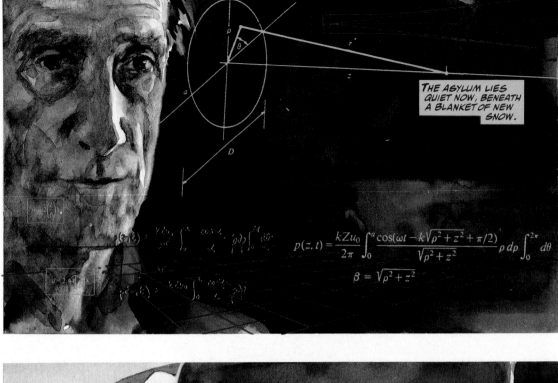

THE ASYLUM LIES QUIET NOW, BENEATH A BLANKET OF NEW SNOW.

$$p(z, t) = \frac{kZu_0}{2\pi} \int_0^a \frac{\cos(\omega t - k\sqrt{\rho^2 + z^2} + \pi/2)}{\sqrt{\rho^2 + z^2}} \rho \, d\rho \int_0^{2\pi} d\theta$$

$$\beta = \sqrt{\rho^2 + z^2}$$

THE BLACK KING AND QUEEN HAVE BEEN LOST.

AN EXCEPTIONAL GAME...

A PITY IT'S OVER. AND YET...

...THERE IS ALWAYS THE ANTICIPATION OF THE GAMES YET TO COME!

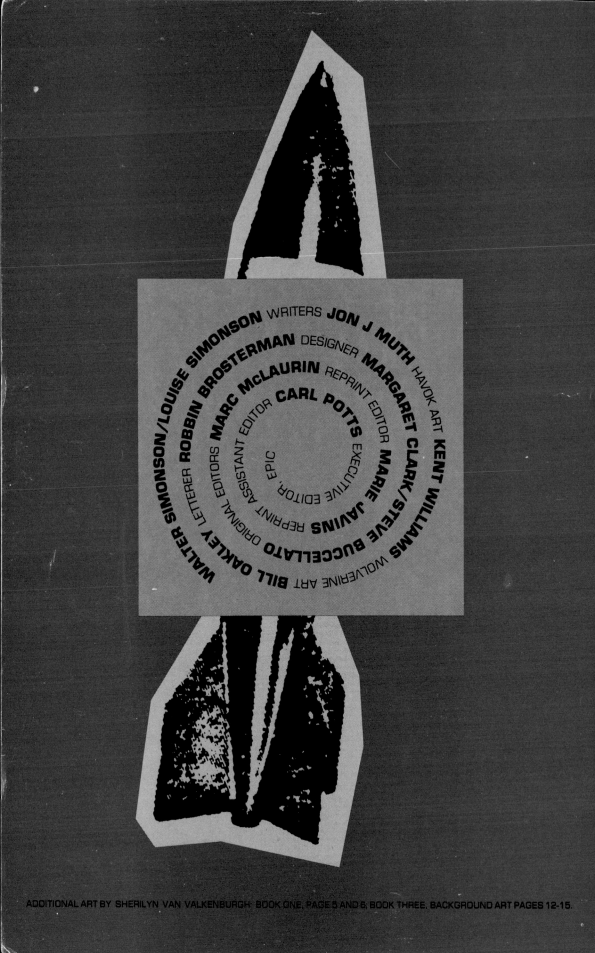

WRITERS **JON J MUTH** / LOUISE SIMONSON / WALTER SIMONSON
HAVOK ART **KENT WILLIAMS**
DESIGNER **MARGARET CLARK** / STEVE BUCCELLATO WOLVERINE ART
REPRINT EDITOR **MARIE JAVINS** REPRINT
EXECUTIVE EDITOR, EPIC **CARL POTTS**
REPRINT ASSISTANT EDITOR **MARC McLAURIN** ORIGINAL EDITORS **BILL OAKLEY** LETTERER **ROBBIN BROSTERMAN**

ADDITIONAL ART BY SHERILYN VAN VALKENBURGH: BOOK ONE, PAGE 5 AND 6; BOOK THREE, BACKGROUND ART PAGES 12-15.